KT-489-158

ASTEROID

Malcolm Rose

Evans

For Faith Wallace

Published by Evans Brothers Limited
2A Portman Mansions
Chiltern St
London W1U 6NR

© Malcolm Rose 2009

First published in 2009

British Library Cataloguing in Publication Data
Rose, Malcolm
    Asteroid. - (Shades)
    1. Young adult fiction
    I. Title
    823.9'14[J]

ISBN-13: 9780237538095

Editor: Julia Moffatt
Designer: Rob Walster

Contents

Chapter One
It's Coming

Josh wasn't paying attention when he rammed the parked car. He should have seen it in plenty of time to drive safely round it but he was staring up at the sky instead of keeping his eyes on the road. And Dave didn't warn him because she had twisted round to watch some men smashing their way into an electrical shop.

Josh and Dave were also unlucky. Modern cars had collision avoidance systems but the old one that they'd stolen didn't. When Josh finally noticed the car in front of him, he was much too close to it. He stamped on the brake pedal and yanked on the steering wheel but it was too late. There was the dreadful sound of crunching metal as air bags blew up in front of them like giant balloons.

Josh's head felt heavy as it rolled forward and then jolted back when the air bag punched him in the face. Like Dave, he felt shocked and winded. But both of them were okay. A car smash was nothing compared to the enormous crash that would happen in six months. A spot of joyriding and a couple of dents would soon be forgotten.

The first community police officer on the scene took one look at them, groaned and took out her pocket computer.

'I don't suppose it's any use asking for your driving licence or insurance. ID cards, please.'

'I haven't got it on me,' Josh said, as if he'd used the line before.

'Nor me,' Dave chimed.

'Mmm. Your names and addresses, then.'

'Joshua Brindle.' Then he dictated his address. He didn't attempt to lie. There was no point.

The officer read the information that had come up on her monitor.

'It says here you're fourteen.'

Josh nodded.

Then it was Dave's turn to give her name. At once, the puzzled officer interrupted. 'Dave?'

'It's short for Davina.'

Josh smiled. Davina didn't look like a

Davina. She was one of the boys. She was a kick-boxing footballer. She didn't look like a Dave either but the name suited her more than Davina did. Josh knew that she preferred Dave because it annoyed her parents and confused just about everyone else.

Whenever Josh thought about girls – which he'd been doing a lot recently – he never thought about Dave. Somehow, she didn't count. That was strange because she was his best friend.

The officer's partner had been talking quietly into his radio. He stepped forward and said, 'This car was stolen about twenty minutes ago. Do you have anything to say about that?'

'Not really,' Josh replied, rubbing his neck where it was sore.

Down the road, a truckload of soldiers

arrived to deal with the disturbance at the phone and computer shop.

The first officer asked, 'Why aren't you in school?'

'No point,' Josh replied. 'A great big asteroid's going to hit the Earth.'

Both of the officers laughed.

'Yeah, yeah. You've been reading too many blogs. Rumours put about by cranks!'

'No. It's coming. And it's going to kill us all.'

The woman shook her head.

'Look. If everyone was about to be wiped off the face of the planet, don't you think we would've been told? It's a conspiracy theory.'

Her partner said, 'When I was at school, the best I came up with was, 'My dog ate my timetable so I didn't know where I was supposed to be'. Bunking off school and nicking cars because the human race is coming to an end – that's a different league.'

The first officer looked up and scanned the clear sky.

'Do you think we've got enough time to take you down to the station or will it strike before we get there?'

The other half of the double act smiled.

'Yeah. We don't want to arrest you if it's not worth filling in the forms.'

On the pavement, an old man sauntered past. He was carrying a sign that read, THE END IS COMING – REPENT YOUR SINS.

The officer with the hand-held computer shook her head again.

'Don't say a word. He's been walking up and down here with the same board for ten years. Hasn't happened yet. He'll probably be at it for the next ten years.'

Josh stared at them. Either they'd been ordered to deny what was going to happen or they'd been told it wasn't true. Josh knew only that his life was being cut short and these people were sharing a joke. 'It *is* coming,' he repeated angrily. 'I know it is.'

It was Josh's mum who drove them away after they'd been cautioned by the police. They sat in silence in the back of the car while she gave them another caution. Looking hassled and annoyed, she finishing the telling-off by muttering, 'I don't know how you could do this to me today of all days.'

'What's special about—?' Joshua stopped. 'Oh, yes. You said. Today's the day the rocket explodes.'

'Yes. Our last chance to save the human race.' Stopping at traffic lights, she glanced at her watch. 'And it'll happen within the hour. I've got to go straight back to work. You can get a bus home. Don't nick another car.'

'Can't we come in and see...?'

'No. Not after what you've just done.'

Josh knew all about the incoming asteroid because his mum worked at the International Spaceguard Centre. She was part of the team trying to nudge the huge lump of rock away from the Earth. Against all the odds, they were trying to avoid total disaster.

'What's this rocket, Mrs Brindle?' Correcting herself, Dave added, 'I mean, Dr Brindle.'

Josh's mum explained, 'It's a multi-megatonne nuclear missile and we launched it from French Guiana weeks ago. It's closing in on the target right now.'

'Will it blast the asteroid to bits?'

'No. We don't have the technology to destroy a rock eight kilometres across. We'll only scratch its surface. But that's the idea – to give it a prod. It might change its course or speed a tiny bit.'

Josh looked at his mother.

'I remember you saying that wouldn't work.'

'I said it probably wouldn't work. But we're desperate so we'll try anything. It's just a shame we didn't do it years ago.'

Josh looked baffled.

'Why?'

'Because it's too close.' His mum changed gear to turn left. 'Think of ten-pin bowling. If the ball swerves a bit just before it hits the front pin, it still makes the strike. But if the angle's slightly wrong when it leaves your hand, it veers off more and more as it rolls down the lane. A little drift becomes a big one over time and it misses most of the

13

pins.' She hesitated and then smiled weakly. 'There's your car crash as well. If you'd seen the parked car soon enough, you could've swerved round it. But you left it too late. You couldn't swerve enough and slammed into it.'

That was something Josh could understand. He nodded.

His mum sighed.

'Pity the Earth hasn't got an air bag to stop us all getting hurt.'

'How big a bomb is it?' Dave asked, always keen to talk about weapons.

'The biggest ever built,' Josh's mum replied. 'You can blast a hole in an asteroid or – like we're doing – explode a bomb just above its surface. Either way, some rock'll get mashed up and blown away. That creates thrust in the opposite direction and knocks it off course. Do you know what I mean? Like when you fire a gun. The bullet goes forward and the gun jerks back. Crumbled rock will fly in one direction, pushing the asteroid in the other.'

She pulled into a parking space outside the International Spaceguard Centre and twisted in her seat.

'Anyway, it depends what the thing's made of. The blast won't be much good if it isn't solid rock. If it's a heap of rubble, it'll be like bombing a sponge. We'll just crush it, not burn it away.' She checked her watch again. 'I'll find out soon.'

Chapter Two

A Cosmic Cannonball

The government hadn't admitted officially that the planet was on a collision course with a large asteroid.

'To stop people panicking,' Josh's mum had explained months ago. 'There's no point announcing what's coming because people can't do anything about it. They can't build shelters or run away from it. It'd be like announcing everyone's going to die. Imagine how they'd react. Riots on the street, binging on drink and drugs, shops would be looted. No one would go to work. Prisoners would smash up prisons and break out. Soldiers would stop fighting each other over bits of the planet. There'd be joyriders everywhere. It'd be chaos. Mind you, a lot of people would suddenly get religion. Churches would fill up.'

In secret, scientists at the International Spaceguard Centre had been trying everything in their power to prevent the collision. But the coming disaster wasn't much of a secret. Rumours were flying around the internet. Joyriders and looters were already on the streets.

Dave went home for tea but Josh felt too restless to go back to an empty house.

Instead, he went to Zack's place. Walking into his friend's bedroom, he said, 'Hi.'

Zack looked up from his desk and the pieces of paper which were covered with scribbled numbers.

'Hi.'

Whenever Josh saw Zack, there was a ritual they went through. Josh always gave him a date test.

'Thirteenth of April 2029.'

With barely a pause, Zack replied, 'That'd be – a Friday.'

Josh laughed. He'd never got used to his friend's frightening maths skills. Ages ago, Josh used to go online to check if Zack had got it right but he didn't bother any more. He'd long since realised that Zack always got it right.

'Friday the thirteenth, eh? Unlucky.'

Josh looked hurt.

'Numbers aren't lucky or unlucky.
They're just – what they are. Sort of pure.'

'Pure? You're a funny guy,' Josh said. 'But
amazing. Talking of unlucky...' He told
Zack about his arrest for a harmless prank
with a car.

Zack shook his head.

'Why do you do it?'

'You've got to do crazy things while
you can.'

'How do you mean?'

It was best to repeat things for Zack. His
brain was weird. It was so full of numbers
and equations that there wasn't room for
anything else.

'The Earth's flying round the sun. So
are a lot of other things.' Josh dropped on
to Zack's bed. 'Some are pretty obvious –
like the rest of the planets – but other stuff
is much smaller. Asteroids. Mum calls

them cosmic cannonballs because their orbits make them smash into planets now and again.'

Zack fiddled with a Rubik's cube while he listened.

'I like orbits. They're circles. Geometry.'

'Yeah. Well. The Earth's been hit by lots of asteroids – and it always will be. Just look at the moon. Lots of craters all over it. It's been bombarded for ages. So's the Earth, but you can't see our craters because of things like trees and plants.'

Zack thought about it for a moment.

'Most of them won't leave craters anyway.'

'How come?'

'Because 71 per cent of the planet's surface is ocean,' Zack said. 'If a hundred cannonballs come at us from all angles, you'd expect 71 of them to hit water. You don't get craters in the sea.'

'Anyway, little ones are pounding us all the time. They burn up in the atmosphere, giving us a firework display. You must have seen shooting stars. Bigger ones – about fifty metres across maybe – aren't so nice. They hit us every two or three hundred years. They get through the atmosphere like the one that blew up above Siberia in 1908. It was as powerful as a thousand atom bombs and trashed two thousand square miles of trees. Lucky! If it had arrived a bit later, it might have flattened London. It would've knocked out everything within the M25 – if they'd had the M25 back then.'

'Impressive,' Zack said.

'When you and me were two, a lump of rock the size of a football pitch—'

Zack shook his head.

'A football pitch is two-dimensional. An

asteroid's three-dimensional. You can't compare them. Maybe it was the size of a football stadium.'

Josh sighed.

'Yeah. I remember now. I was lying in my cot, thinking it's as big as a football stadium. It was going at 23 thousand miles per hour and it missed us by a few thousand miles. Just imagine. That would've made a mess.'

'Was that the biggest?'

'No. Ones about a kilometre across hit the planet every hundred thousand years. Real whoppers – over six kilometres – crash down every hundred million years or so. Mum says a four-kilometre asteroid would kill half the world's population. Bigger than that and they'd wipe out civilisation, maybe all life. That's what did in the dinosaurs.'

'Yeah?'

'A ten-kilometre asteroid hit Mexico
65 million years ago. Not that it was called
Mexico then. It heated the air so much that
whole continents burst into flames. Like
paper under a magnifying glass. Forests and
everything got burnt up in the firestorm and
the dust blotted out the sun so no plants
could grow. No food. And there were giant
waves that flooded lots of places. It was like
every kind of environmental disaster rolled
into one. A mega-disaster.'

Zack twisted several faces of his Rubik's
cube in turn and all of the colours fell
speedily into place.

'It must've hit rock to do all that. If it came
down in the sea, it'd just make a big splash.'

'A splash!' Josh cried. 'One that size
would make waves over a hundred metres
high, according to Mum. They'd swamp the

land and drown everything in their way.'

'That's some cannonball.'

'Yeah. And we're overdue a big one.'

Zack shrugged.

'Scientists – like your mum – will stop it hitting us.'

'She's trying right now but—' Josh was sure his mum thought that the final attempt to save the planet wouldn't work.

'They'll send what's-his-name up with a big bomb.'

Puzzled, Josh asked, 'Who?'

'It was in a movie ages ago.'

'Bruce Willis, you mean? He went up in a rocket and nuked one to bits. Can't remember what the film was called.'

'That's it.'

Josh smiled.

'Not a good idea. The bits will keep coming, Mum says. Like turning a cannonball into a cluster bomb. We'll be hammered by lots of small chunks instead of one big one. And the nuke will have made them radioactive. Anyway, the one that's on its way is too big to blast apart. On top of that, she hasn't got Bruce Willis's phone number.'

'Pity,' Zack said.

Chapter Three
NEO 2003 XF17

Josh's mum was right. The most powerful
weapon ever built by human beings
exploded alongside the incoming asteroid
and gave it a sideways shove that was too
weak to alter its destiny. The obstinate rock
would smash into a different part of the
planet but the result would be the same. The
Earth's last chance had ended in failure.

Josh and Zack had been friends ever since they'd met at school and found out that they'd been born on the same day. Not just any old day. They were both born on 1st January 2000. Making his appearance 23 seconds after midnight, Josh was the first baby in Britain to be born in the 21st century. But he guessed that the hospital had fiddled it so they could get the publicity. Zack was way down the list. He wasn't born until the new dawn.

Josh had talked to Zack about the incoming asteroid before. Zack had believed every word but hadn't taken much notice because he wasn't really interested. Only one thing really grabbed his attention: maths. At school, his marks in all of the other subjects made him out to be an idiot. But he wasn't because the teachers said he was doing maths beyond university level. Zack was part dunce, part genius.

'I'll tell you what happened,' Josh said, propping himself up on his elbows. 'A few years ago, Mum's outfit spotted a big near-Earth object. That's what they call asteroids that are coming our way. NEOs. Because they saw this one in 2003, they called it 2003 XF17.'

'Nice name.' Zack wasn't joking.

'You only like it because it's got numbers in it. I don't think it's much of a name. They could've called it Earth Slayer, Doomsday, or something exciting like Peter. It shot past pretty close six years ago. Mum got annoyed with me because she showed me this boring light moving across the sky and I was more interested in a plane with flashing lights. Anyway, they worked its orbit out. Mum said the chances of it hitting us this year were only one in nineteen thousand.'

Zack interrupted. 'People do the lottery but the odds of winning the big one are less than that.'

'Yeah, but the trouble is, when it went past in 2008, it was affected by Earth's gravity. Its course and speed got changed. Just a bit, she said. But it was enough to put it on a collision course this time around. They know because it came close enough for them to send a rocket up and attach a radio transmitter. They've been tracking its exact position ever since. Now they know it'll hit. That's when Mum stopped smiling at babies.'

'You what?'

'She used to smile at babies – anyone's babies, even the really ugly ones – but she doesn't now. She just looks sad.'

'So, how big is this asteroid?'

'Not much smaller than the dinosaurs'.

Cockroaches and stuff will be all right but it'll wipe the human race out – and almost everything else that's alive.'

'If it comes down on land,' Zack added.

'Yeah. If it hits the sea, it'll only kill tens of millions of people.' Josh gazed at his strange friend. 'So, what are you going to do, Zack?'

'What can I do? I can't catch it and chuck it back into space, can I?'

'No. I mean, what are you going to do before the end of the world?'

He shrugged.

'I'd like to work out a formula for prime numbers.'

Josh didn't understand.

'You're a maths junkie. There should a clinic that'd help you kick the habit. What about *living*?'

'How do you mean?'

'Well, girls and sex come to mind. You can't help wondering what all the fuss is about, can you?'

Zack turned up his nose.

'It sounds a bit – messy and embarrassing. And unlikely.'

'Just you wait. When someone official tells what's happening, girls will be really up for it.'

'Mmm.'

Josh wasn't put off by Zack's frosty reaction.

'There's lots of things. Most of it's against the law. Nicking whatever you want, driving, going to gigs, drink. Binging on anything, really.'

'Okay. I'll binge on numbers,' Zack decided.

'Boring. When I got into trouble, Mum used to say, 'Well, you've gone and done it now and you'll suffer the consequences.' She doesn't any more. There aren't any consequences. Think about it. There's time to get down and dirty but not enough to find yourself in trouble. The law doesn't move that quickly. And neither do girls. No one gives birth in six months. And you don't have to worry about picking up diseases.'

Zack simply shook his head.

'Nobody'll turn up for school. Except you. Not even teachers. What's the point? XF17 doesn't care if it kills kids who are good at algebra or not.'

'If you're right,' Zack said thoughtfully, 'and everybody cops it, you'll be the oldest person in the country to be born and die in this century.'

Josh sighed.

'That sure makes me feel a whole lot better.'

Chapter Four
Poke it with a Stick

Josh stared in disbelief at his computer screen.

'Arrgh!' he cried. 'I can't believe you did that!'

Dave laughed.

'Well, I did. How are you going fight me now? I've blasted your weapons to pieces.'

Josh thought he was the king of War Game.

'But I'd buried them way down in an underground bunker.'

Davina shrugged.

'Not deep enough for my bunker-busting bombs.'

'That's mean.'

'Game over.' Dave raised her arms in victory.

Josh and Dave were playing games because they didn't want to think about the news that Josh's mum might bring home. They didn't want to hear the worst.

'Right,' Josh said. 'Let's play again.'

Before the game reached its conclusion, they were interrupted by the front door opening and closing downstairs.

At once, they stopped playing and looked at each other in silence.

Then Josh nodded towards the door. 'That'll be Mum. We'd better...'

Dave followed him downstairs.

The space scientists had thrown all of their technology at 2003 XF17 in an attempt to budge it off course but it hadn't even blinked. It was continuing its collision course with the Earth, certain to cause mass extinction of all higher life forms.

But the event wasn't very important in a restless and uncaring universe. Compared to the death of a star, it wouldn't even be spectacular. It would hardly cause a blip in the grand scheme of things. Human beings were the only ones who cared.

'The explosion changed its speed by a few centimetres per second. That's all.' Worn out, Josh's mum slumped onto the sofa with a cup of tea. Judging by the smell, she'd added a large slug of alcohol. 'It'd miss the Earth if we had five or ten years to wait. But we've only got six months. We might as well have poked it with a stick.' She paused for a drink before adding, 'I'm sorry. I think it's too late. I think impact's unavoidable. I don't know what else we can do. Some of my colleagues have given up. They say the only thing to do is go home, wait, pray and prepare.'

Dave asked, 'What have you done so far?'

Mum took a deep breath.

'Ages ago, we attached rocket boosters to shunt it to new course. A bit like a tugboat pulling a great big ship. It's working. It's shifted the orbit by a fraction of a millimetre but it'll take years to change it enough to avoid us. We don't have that luxury. We stuck a large solar sail on its surface as well. The solar wind will steer it off track but it looks like that needs even longer – a century or so.' She sighed. 'The team even talked about painting it.'

'What?' Josh exclaimed.

'It's not as daft as it sounds. You paint half of it black and that side would absorb more heat from the sun. That'd change the way it moves. Or you could paint it silver to reflect sunlight, cooling half of it down. Again, that'd affect its path. It might work if we could wait decades for the change to happen.'

'Crazy,' Josh muttered.

'There's plenty more crazy stuff where that came from. You could capture a small asteroid in Earth's orbit and then use the slingshot effect to catapult it at XF17. Think of it as a game of billiards – with civilisation as the stake. This is one shot you don't want to get wrong. You'd have to hit the incoming asteroid in precisely the right place, at the right angle and speed.

But it's a half-baked idea. We won't have that technology ready in time.'

'What else is there?'

She shrugged helplessly.

'You could use a high-power laser to burn a hole in it and the stream of vaporised rock would turn it into a sort-of rocket. But we'd need time to develop the method and then another ten years for the push to make it miss the Earth.'

Dave nodded slowly.

'If I get this right, you need to blast a bigger hole in it to get more oomph.'

'Yes. More pulverised rock means more thrust.'

'So,' Dave said, 'you ought to do what I've just done to Josh.'

'What do you mean?'

'It's not rocket science, is it? Well, yes, that's exactly what it is. Use bunker buster bombs.'

Josh butted in.

'They only exist in a computer game!'

'No,' Dave replied. 'They're real. The Americans make the best ones. They can go through 50 metres of concrete or more before they go boom.'

'They must be top secret,' said Josh.

Davina laughed.

'Not exactly. They're in Wikipedia. They're meant to blow up weapons of mass destruction when the bad guys bury them underground.'

They both turned towards Josh's mum.

She had frozen. She was staring silently into her spiced-up tea. Then she looked up at them. Her face was flushed with excitement. 'You know, that's—' She reached for the phone.

Chapter Five

Death Star set to Destroy Earth

Outside, a siren suddenly stopped screaming as a police car came to a halt by the scene of the latest burglary.

Dr Brindle was trying to explain to her son why Dave's idea hadn't yet got off the ground. 'You see, we're having to deal with – sensitivities.'

'What does that mean?' Josh cried.

'It means America doesn't want to reveal all about its bunker buster technology to everyone in Spaceguard. It includes Russia, the Middle East and—'

'What?' Josh exploded. 'Remind them that we're talking about the end of the world here. If they don't play the team game, there won't be any bunkers to bust. They won't have any enemies to keep secrets from or drop bombs on.'

'Yes, but we still have to tread carefully. If we survive XF17, they'll have given away a lot of military secrets.'

'Who cares?'

'America.'

Josh threw up his hands in disgust.

'We're having to persuade China to play ball as well. They've developed a new rocket that could carry the bomb. Nuclear pulse propulsion. It's super-fast so it'd reach the asteroid far quicker than a normal rocket and transfer much more kinetic energy—' She stopped, realising that she was getting too technical. 'It'd deliver a bunker buster at unbelievable speed so even a launch this late might succeed. *Might*, not *will*. But the bomb would pack a huge punch that'd hollow out a lot of rock. It stands a chance. There's a couple of problems. The rocket's experimental. When it lifts off there'll be radioactive fallout that'll cause a few deaths on the ground. But I suppose it's a good deal compared with wiping everyone out. And China will have to share its hush-hush technology with the US.'

'Talking of hush-hush,' Josh said, 'you're not going to like this.'

'What?'

He held up the front page of the *Daily Star* that he'd stolen from the library. The headline shrieked.

So did Josh's mum when she saw it. *'Death Star Set To Destroy Earth! Rumours Confirmed.* How did they...? It wasn't supposed to get in the papers!' She grabbed the article from Josh. 'And what's it got to do with a star? It's an asteroid.'

'Death Star sounds good,' Josh said. 'I mean, it's the shock-horror tactic. No one'll believe it. It's the *Daily Star*.' Josh paused and then added, 'That's probably why they've put *star*.'

His mum was reading too frantically to react to his wit. Eventually, she looked up. 'Every journalist will be on to it now. It'll be all over the telly tonight.'

'At least people'll know what's coming, if they didn't already know.'

His mum shook her head sadly. 'It won't do them any good. It'll be a disaster.'

'Not as big a disaster as the asteroid.'

The authorities knew they couldn't keep the story secret for ever. Sooner or later, someone in the know would leak the story, journalists would break the ban on news coverage, or amateur astronomers would spot XF17 with their telescopes.

Now it had happened, the government declared a state of emergency and doubled the police officers, dog handlers, soldiers and army vehicles patrolling the streets, trying to maintain order.

It was an impossible job. In town centres, windows were broken and shops emptied of anything valuable or useful. A gig in Leicester developed into a riot and two people were killed in the fighting. On stage, the musicians trashed their instruments. They didn't need them any more.

Hospitals began to empty. The terminally ill were sent home to die among their loved ones. Relatives of patients on life support went into the wards to say their tearful farewells and wonder when it was best to turn off the machines. A lot of medical staff went home to their own families.

In church, a preacher told her congregation that God would produce a miracle or that He would allow the faithful few to take to an ark just before the seas rose up and engulfed the land.

Round the back of the church, between the ancient gravestones, a boy and a girl who had just met were touching each other eagerly but clumsily. Afraid that they might be disturbed or caught, they hesitated every time they heard a noise. A vehicle crashing, a window smashing, the sound of gunshots, the pounding of footsteps, someone screaming and swearing, a siren blaring.

In the run-up to XF17, this was what life had become.

Chapter Six
The Hopes of the Human Race

'Okay,' Josh's mum said brightly. 'It's game on.'

For a moment Josh looked puzzled, then he replied, 'You mean, America and China have got their act together?'

'Yes. With European navigation experts. The best team we've got. And the last chance we've got.'

'Go for it!'

'That's not all.'

'Oh?'

'I got permission for you and Davina to come in and watch the launch. If you want. The bunker buster was her idea.'

Josh stared at his mum.

'You're launching it in Leicester?'

She laughed.

'No. The Gobi desert, China. But we'll have it live on a giant screen. And you'll hear everything.'

'Fantastic!' Then he stopped to think.

'What's up?'

'Can I bring Zack as well? He'd love it.'

She shrugged. 'I don't see why not. But no more.'

'Wow!' Dave uttered as she gazed at the

rocket on the screen. 'It's a monster! Not like the space shuttle.'

'That's because it's not burning ordinary rocket fuel,' Josh's mum said. 'It's nuclear powered.'

Josh was open-mouthed.

'*That's* what our lives depend on?'

His mum nodded.

'Yes. It's the only rocket of its kind. The only one with the speed to save us. It's do-or-die time.' One of her colleagues called her over so she said to Josh and his friends, 'You stay here.' Then she went to her workstation.

Between the visitors' gallery and the huge screen showing live pictures from China there were rows and rows of long benches. Almost all of the experts in the Spaceguard control room were sitting in front of computer monitors. From unseen ghostly voices, mostly Chinese accents. It ms were coming up to actly as planned. e screen for a few seconds but he was more interested in the pages and pages of calculations that he saw on the end of one of the desks. While everyone else eyed the rocket, he was scanning the dense lines of figures.

Josh felt his heart beating faster as if he were part of the team rather than simply watching helplessly. For some reason, he found himself clutching Dave's hand.

A voice declared, 'Ready for countdown. The hopes of the human race rest on this mission.'

At once, the room hushed and the tension went through the roof.

Josh felt like a sprinter, straining in his

blocks, heart pounding, waiting for the starter's pistol. After six agonising minutes of delay, a distant Chinese voice began, 'Ten, nine, eight...'

The seconds seemed so slow.

Josh was holding his breath. The rest of his life depended on the untested rocket and the unusual bomb that it was carrying.

'...seven, six, five...'

There was a disturbance in the room.

It was Zack. He was waving the pages of calculations and shouting.

'Hey! Stop! You want to see this!'

Everyone turned round and stared at him as he began to run towards the centre of the control room.

'...four, three...'

Josh's mum looked embarrassed. A boy she'd brought to the centre was making a fool of himself at a vital point in human history. The other workers simply looked annoyed. A huge security officer intercepted him. 'You can't come over here. Keep to the visitors' gallery.'

'No! You've got to stop—'

'...two, one...'

Zack's face was a mixture of fear and fury. He yelled at Josh's mum, 'Listen to me! There's a mistake...'

The security guy had him by the arms and began to march him towards the exit.

'...zero, lift off!'

The giant rocket seemed to hesitate and then rose majestically into the air. It seemed slow at first but, as it climbed, it quickly gathered speed. After only a few seconds, it was up in the clouds and the Spaceguard staff clapped and cheered.

Not Dr Brindle. She rushed after Zack. So did Josh and Dave. They all came together by the main door.

'What's going on?' Josh's mum cried.

Zack wriggled out of the bouncer's grip.

'These calculations are amazing. So complicated. I can't follow them. But I know a glitch when I see one.'

Josh's mum paused for a moment and then laughed. 'You've got to be joking, Zack. They've been examined by all our experts. By the Americans and Chinese as well.'

'That's the problem,' said Zack. 'Too many different people.' He stared at the big screen. The spacecraft was out of shot, well beyond the cloud. 'But it's too late! You've just ruined—'

'No, Zack. The maths have been checked and re-checked. You can't possibly – You're just a school kid.'

Zack glanced at Josh and Dave for support as the security officer grabbed him again.

Josh had only a moment to decide who to trust: a whole gang of experts or his young friend.

'Wait!' he said. 'If Zack says there's a problem, there's a problem.'

'Yeah. That's right,' Dave put in.

'Mum!' Josh shouted.

'All right,' she said to the bouncer. 'Let me talk to him.'

Chapter Seven
Live or Die

The four of them were sitting round a table covered in the pages of Spaceguard's calculations. It reminded Josh of being in Zack's bedroom where scribbled numbers always littered his desk.

'I don't know what half of this means,' Zack said, waving his hand at the sheets of paper. 'But look. This bit's about geometry—'

Josh's mum interrupted.

'The rocket trajectory.'

'Yes. It's in metres, right?'

'Yes.'

'So, where does it get converted into imperial units: feet and inches?'

Josh's mum looked puzzled.

'Why should it? We always work in metric.'

Zack rustled the papers as he searched hurriedly for the one he wanted. When he found it, he slapped it down in front of her.

'This is about the bomb...'

She butted in again.

'That's from the American spacecraft engineers.'

'Here, see. The thrust. It's in pounds-seconds. Pounds! That's not metric.'

Josh's mum went back through the figures. Finally taking Zack seriously, she muttered to herself, 'We calculated thrust in newton-seconds.' Astounded, she looked up at Zack. 'You're right.'

Josh exchanged a puzzled glance with Dave and then asked, 'What does it mean?'

His mum's face was utterly white.

'I'm going to have to call in the engineers and check the main computer but it looks like the rocket's got numbers from America in the wrong units.'

'So what?'

'The rocket thrust will be wrong. It'd be like trying to hit a target three metres off the ground by aiming three feet high. The rocket will release the bomb in the wrong place or miss the asteroid altogether! I don't know how it could've happened. It's a school kid error.'

Zack looked offended.

'I wouldn't have made it!'

She put her hand on his arm.

'Sorry, Zack.'

'Never mind that,' Dave said. 'What can you do about it? Has someone ruined my idea? Is it too late?'

'I don't know,' Josh's mum replied. 'I need to go and see the software people. *Now.*'

When Josh's mum returned, she wasn't so pale. She even smiled.

'They did it! They've reprogrammed the onboard computer before it got too far away.'

'It knows its feet from its metres now?' Zack checked.

Relieved, she slumped into a chair.

'Thanks to you, yes.'

'So the bunker buster's back on track?' Dave asked.

She nodded.

'It'll blast into the asteroid exactly where

we calculated. Between you, you might just have saved the world.'

Josh, Dave and Zack smiled proudly at each other. Josh said, 'What do we do now?'

His mum shrugged.

'We wait. And hope.'

'Is that all?'

'There's nothing else. We wait to see if we've done enough. We wait to find out if we're going to live or die.'

Author Note

Asteroid 2003 XF17 is fictional. All other asteroids in this story are real.

There are many rocks on a collision course with the Earth, but none of them is similar in size to the asteroid that struck the planet and wiped out the dinosaurs. Most are small enough to be harmless. Perhaps the biggest threat is the asteroid 2004 MN4 (also called Apophis) which will swing past the Earth on Friday 13th April 2029. It is about 320 metres across and it will be visible as a point of light moving across the sky. It will not collide with the planet in 2029 but it will come close enough for Earth's gravity to change its velocity and orbit slightly. It is not yet known if this change will make a future collision more or less likely but there is the possibility of an impact when 2004 MN4 returns on Friday 13th April 2035 and again in April 2036. There are other risk dates in this century and an overall chance of 1 in 6000 that MN4 will strike the Earth on one of these fly-bys. It is not large enough to threaten us with extinction but a collision would cause regional devastation. It could take out a major city if it hit land or quite a few coastal cities if it plunged into the sea and triggered tsunamis.

In 1999, the Mars Climate Orbiter smashed into the surface of Mars or burnt up in the planet's atmosphere rather than going smoothly into the planned orbit 150 kilometres above the surface. This happened because of an error of units. Navigation experts who work out rocket paths measured thrust in the metric unit of newton-seconds but spacecraft engineers worked in the imperial unit of pound-seconds. The spacecraft's software thought that the numbers supplied were in newton-seconds rather than pound-seconds with the result that the orbiter went far too close to Mars when it tried to go into orbit. That simple mathematical error wrecked a £65 million project.

Are you a maths junkie?

1) In which year does the action in the story take place? (The year is not given explicitly but it can be calculated.)

2) Name some imperial units in everyday use.

3) Name some metric units in everyday use.

4) Convert 23,000 mph to kilometres per second.

5) If an asteroid travelling at 23,000 mph is 115.92 million miles away, how many weeks have we got before it strikes?

6) There's a 1 in 500 chance of winning a prize. Express this as a percentage.

7) There's a 1 in 6000 chance of MN4 striking the Earth. Express this as a percentage.

8) Name objects that are in orbit around the Sun.

9)   Name objects that are in orbit around the Earth.

10) In one year the Earth moves around the Sun at an approximate distance of 93 million miles. What distance does the Earth travel in one orbit? At what speed is it moving?

11) In this story, Zack objects when Josh compares a football pitch (measured in area units of square metres) with a three-dimensional asteroid (measured in cubic metres). Environmentalists often urge us to have a shower rather than a bath because showers use less water. What is wrong with these comparisons?